Things Remote...

A Love Letter

to

Newfoundland

First edition September 2025

ISBN-10: 978-1-952833-68-7
ISBN-13: 1-952833-68-X

Things Remote...

A Love Letter
to
Newfoundland

"As for me, I am tormented with an everlasting itch for things remote . . ."
Herman Melville, Moby-Dick or, The Whale.

A fictionalized story inspired by true events...

Emma Winters

TJS PUBLISHING HOUSE

DEDICATION

From the moment you entered my life, you brought endless joy and love. Keep following your dreams with passion, knowing that I will always stand by your side, so proud of you, cheering you on.

CONTENTS

ACKNOWLEDGMENTS

First of all, my thanks to the wonderful people of Newfoundland who made this story possible. Your warmth and hospitality make Newfoundland a place of welcome and beauty one can never forget.

I'd also like to thank my editor, Nicole Hayes, at JHWritingPlus for all her help and expertise. The book is better because of her contributions and the insights she provided. Blessings!

My thanks to Christel Franken, as well, Head of Development at The Garden Cinema in London, England for her time, affection and support, especially during the early stages of writing.

I'd also like to give my deepest appreciation to Drew Logan, gifted actor and writer, who appeared as an angel from the sky to offer guidance and motivation at just the right time. Thank you, Drew!

Finally, thanks to my dear sister, who offered words of encouragement, love and support, despite her busy schedule. My warmest thanks to Amber for her kindness, care and enthusiasm in all she did and equally to her sister Michelle, two of the loveliest people one could ever hope to meet.

And with grateful love, my thanks to my parents; my father in particular, for his embracing support of my chosen field in film and television, and who taught me, by example, the joy of creativity and of writing. He wrote the most amazing stories, and wrote, unfailingly, every single day of his life.

But, my deepest love and appreciation goes to my son, for the wonderment and joy he has brought into my life, for his love, intelligence and insight. He is truly a gift from the Lord. Dearest son, I wish you happiness and fulfillment in all you do. Have faith and always follow your dreams.

THINGS REMOTE . . .

A Love Letter to Newfoundland

"As for me, I am tormented with an everlasting itch for things remote . . ."

Herman Melville, Moby- Dick or, the Whale.

A fictionalized story inspired by true events...

Prologue

A howling wind whips through the streets of St. John, this remote, far-away Newfoundland town, bringing with it a relentless onslaught of snow. As I look below from my hotel window, I see a tempest of epic proportions, a blizzard that has transformed this picturesque landscape with its majestic icebergs floating in the distance into a treacherous, frozen arctic. The snow has risen with such fury that it threatens to engulf our very hotel. I am on the fifth floor, and the snow is rising like a flood tide, more snow than has ever been seen in 166 years of recorded history.

As an acting and dialect coach in film and television, I've had a wonderful, unique, and all-consuming experience. I have traveled all over the world studying and teaching, but with all my traveling, I have never been in a country or town that has resonated with me as the province of Newfoundland has. There is something magical here that has stayed with me for a long time. It's as though I've been thrown back to an ancient time. And, more importantly, from what I can see, the people of Newfoundland show great resilience while possessing an endearing warmth belying the rigors of their harsh reality, and it touches the heart.

The Newfoundland accent is not something often heard in film. Also, there are a few variations of this accent depending on the origins of their ancestors. I have worked with a variety of actors—both 'A-listers' and newcomers— and on this particular project, I am very excited for both the challenge and to be working with some of the actors I've worked with previously.

I have been hired to ensure the authenticity of the actors' accents. I've traveled quite a distance for this particular film project to understand the how and why of the culture: the way they live and speak, and the history of this fascinating place. I try to immerse myself in the culture on various film projects whenever I can.

The town I intended to fly into to do my specific research on the Irish side of the island was to be my final destination for my trip. The airport—my only escape—was buried beneath a thick blanket of white. It would have been impossible to fly on a chartered plane in these conditions, so the reservation had to be cancelled immediately. So much for my research trip.

The year is 2002, a challenging time in the world, especially in the United States, where there had never been an attack on our soil before. Until this time, no country or group had ever dared attack us. But seeing the Twin Towers in New York City fall last September forced many of us to realize we were entering a new world, a world where life would never be quite the same. Yet, as I got to know these Newfoundlanders and listened to their stories, I learned about strength and resilience from a people filled with hope and national pride. It was a healing balm for my soul and an unexpected surprise.

To continue with the story, as the saying goes, when one door closes, another one opens. News of my predicament spread like wildfire throughout the hotel and in the town of St. John. Within the hour, hotel staff and townspeople rallied together, filled with a collective determination to help me in my quest for the research I needed for the film, despite the weather and its restrictions. They formed a human chain, as it were, coming up to my room one by one, or in small groups— some given permission to be there during working hours, others offering their time generously before or after work.

The hotel staff and others immersed themselves in my cause. Weather was not a deterrent to these Newfoundlanders. Instead, they dug deep, unearthing stories of forgotten lore and of a rich history that whispered of the secrets of this mysterious island, this Newfoundland. I could see the joy in their eyes at the telling of each story. With each memory or bit of history they shared, their recollections grew with excitement and were told with swelling provincial pride.

But what surprised me even more was that the generosity of this community did not stop there. The next day and beyond, with the continuing weather conditions and limitations, these Newfoundlanders opened up their homes, embracing me with warm hearts and hearths, offering me cups of tea as the scent of soup and freshly baked bread wafted through the air as a testament to their welcoming hospitality. As we gathered around each table, their stories unfolded like a tapestry, weaving together the fabric of their lives into the history of this resilient province. I recorded their stories, the way they spoke, the subtle nuances, their turn of a phrase, or a particular ancient sound of the Celtics that had traveled through history, and its winsome lilt and music that whispered of treasures of the seas from so long ago.

In the face of adversity, this town became my sanctuary away from the biting wind and snow. As the snow reached heights that defied reason, the spirits of these locals soared even higher as they delved deeper into the telling of their unique history and culture and brought it to life. Finally, I was armed and ready to work. Snow be damned. Filming was about to begin.

CHAPTER 1

I am in Newfoundland, April 2002, just after the attacks on the World Trade Center. I wrap my woolen scarf around my face as quickly as I can as I stand on the cold moon. But no, not really; it only seems as though I am standing on the moon because where else could I be so foreign? There is more snow on the ground than there has been in 166 years. The moon-like mountains and craters look untouched in the vast expanse. My boots crunch in the snow as I sink, footsteps marring the pure landscape. I look behind me and think, as Neil Armstrong did, *Will someone come one day and clean these up?* I have landed on an isolated planet.

The night drive to the house, where we are billeted, puzzles me as roads rise up and drop without warning. A curve comes up suddenly, and I grip the door handle as we swerve to the left. *Who were the engineers who designed these roads?* I wonder. It's like being on a rollercoaster ride.

"Yes, b'y, moose is what you gotta watch out for," says the driver, cutting through my thoughts in his Newfoundland accent.

Nodding by way of comfort, he adds, "They got big bodies and spindly legs. Many a driver has been taken by surprise at the sight of a huge body crashin' through the windshield."

I'm not comforted.

"'Oh, God,' are often the last words spoken," he continues, prophetically.

Would I have time for those last words—or any—if I encounter a moose head on? I wonder to myself.

As we round a corner, a breathtakingly large harvest moon appears over the next hill. I gasp. It's so big that there is a face on it. I will swear to that. The Harvest Moon smiles at me, welcoming me. I smile back but grip the handle again, glancing furtively at the driver while bracing myself for the next surprise.

There is no door to the house. Well, there *is* a door, but it is hidden beneath eleven feet of snow. We trudge around to the back, hoping for better luck. The wind and snow battle with us as the driver pulls my arm almost out of its socket in an attempt to get me to the back of the house without losing me in the elements. We make it, and the door, protected by a life-saving overhang as though designed for such a surreal moment as this, opens. I breathe a sigh of relief.

"Yes, b'y, we made it!" Welcome to Newfoundland.

Collections of spoons appear in every room, standing like shiny soldiers ready to serve. Each wall is painted a different color, and each rug a mismatched hue. I am an explorer in a white-encrusted, rainbow cave where my ancestors painted figures on cave walls each night. The human spirit's need for color and life is in full bloom here. There is no hiding it there. Living in the harsh reality of a northern winter for eight, nine months out of the year, there appears to be a need—a yearning—for life and color.

Outside, the roofs of each house are painted different colors as well, so that men can find their way home at the end of a workday. Under the vast, blinding white and months of heavy snow, these men would otherwise be lost. Colors are their lighthouses, beckoning them safely home under star-filled nights as long as they remember their paint color!

The next morning, after breakfast, we venture out cautiously. The weather has calmed somewhat from the flurries and wind of the night before.

Amber, my eighteen-year-old niece and temporary nanny, in her white-fleeced snowsuit, stands bright against the snow, her dark, red hair and its explosion of curls framing a snow-queen face. The contrast of color against a snowy wilderness is lovely as she laughs and plays with my eight-year-old son, Noah, watching him with tender care. I watch Noah running in the snow, waving his arms while seagulls follow him in the air. A red fox peeks out and scampers behind him in the distance, hoping to play with him, too. These are the moments in my mind, frozen in time, where the landscape of nature is rich and full, even in the cold of winter.

Other children go running to play outside, too: caged birds set free, cawing wild and strong, as parents shout, "Don't sit on 'dem telephone wires!" That's how high the snow is this winter, seemingly meeting up with the sky, up to the telephone wires. But the children, not heeding, sit on the wires, then soar through the air, and tumble down through the snow, until suddenly, they disappear. Some fall deep, deep down into the snow. Alarms are raised; firemen are called. Newfoundland knights in red and white jump off their trucks and leap to the rescue, thrusting long javelins into the snow until "something soft" is felt—a child, buried many feet below, waiting to be rescued.

We get ready with things we must do before work begins and prepare excitedly for my son's first day of school. There is one school for several towns in the area that invites hundreds of children of all ages. My son is thrilled to be with such welcoming children as they encircle him with warmth and childlike curiosity. He is a seashell-treasured Robinson Crusoe discovery, delivered upon the shores of their island for their delight. I am happy to see him so excited as he is led down the hall amidst laughter and giggles. I smile as I watch him go, then turn to look for Amber. Half of the young men in the school surround her, drawn like magnets. Her snow-queen face lights up, eyes twinkling, coquettish red curls bouncing in the soft, northern light. She is holding court. The days of my youth flood back, and I relive them in this moment. It is good to be alive.

I didn't realize the school offered art until the last period, when I went to pick up my son that afternoon. I am directed to the art room down the hall at the end of a long corridor. The art teacher, James Murphy, is helping

Noah with an art project he will need to do to catch up with the others. Noah and the teacher are focused on the creation of mixing colors on the palette. The art teacher takes some paint and brushes and shows my son the various changing hues. As he hands Noah a brush to try the landscape, I look at the art teacher's profile. He is a Botticelli with dark curls, green eyes, and long dark eyelashes, rising out of the sea, a painting in and of itself. My breath catches. With each passing moment, I am falling more and more in love with Newfoundland.

Tongue-tied, I turn away to look around the art room. There is artwork from students of all ages. Some have painted pictures of houses in water floating away with a caption above that reads, "Resettlement, 1953." I can feel James watching me as I look. It seems students are learning about the Newfoundland and Labrador government resettlement of 1953 and beyond. The peril of houses, schools, churches, towns, and villages disappearing from beneath their feet teaches children of the uncertainty of life.

I glance back at this beautiful Renaissance man as he guides my son's hand with the paintbrush. The strokes are steady, firm. But the pictures on the wall tell a different story. The lines in those paintings are shaky, undefined. There is no permanency. A house is tipped on its side as it travels across the water. People and animals follow a funeral pyre of wooden sacrifices of beds, chairs, and tables to be offered on the altar of the government gods. I turn back to him again, eyes searching, then away.

Pointers in hand, I see depictions of government men marking counties and islands on a worn world map throughout the ages. "You take this. I'll take that." Puppet people on a string moved from town to town. A line on the map is drawn in ink and blood, centuries old. I can feel James watching my movements as I walk and look. Color rising. I want to stay in this room forever. I feel a powerful undercurrent pass between us.

The pictures cry out as entitlement echoes throughout the mega-horn of time, where homes and communities are doomed, reduced to wandering refugees from land to land. These are the lessons to be learned and the lessons we must teach our young. Government officials retrace a map, changing the world—home and hearth be damned—drinking sweet coffee sprinkled with satisfaction. Around the world, they place and displace people and towns throughout the ages *"Move my village from here to here. I won't care. I'm invisible." "This was never a country...look at these barbarians...no one here with feelings. You have no feeling, only I have feeling."* It is the same story throughout the ages. I turn back to look at the art teacher's face, needing, instead, to look at present beauty and promise.

James comes close and we stand for a moment, awkward as children on their first day of school. Sea green eyes envelope me. Lips, fingertips tingle, messages unspoken.

Our breath mingles in shy accord as we head back to the art table. My son is creating an innocent sunrise over dark, blue waters. My thoughts of James spin around in my head—innocent and not-so-innocent thoughts—creating confusion and excitement.

CHAPTER 2

I begin work early the next morning while it is still dark. Fighting wind and snow, the driver and I battle to reach the car and pull the doors open with every bit of our strength. We laugh a little laugh of victory as we tumble into the car, exhausted, and the day has only just begun.

When we arrive, the crew is standing around like fools watching the swirling snow mount higher and higher, enveloping us. There will be no work today. The locals look at us, laughing among themselves. It's good that they are laughing and standing around, getting paid for nothing. Work here had been scarce since the Turbot War of 1995. Cod, a staple of Newfoundland, has now been declared an endangered species. Whereas once you could walk from boat to boat and "not get your feet wet" as plentiful fish could be relied upon to yield an endless supply, it has now become a barren sea, yielding instead poverty and lack. The heavy government nets cast two hundred miles offshore years ago, trapping the fish, have made sure of that. *Oh, Canada, land that I love . . .*

The next day, we begin filming again, in earnest, on top of a cliff. A house had been moved up there for the filming, and a road had been built expressly for us to gain access to this isolated location. The house sits in the glow of the morning sun upon the rugged terrain. It is a land where nature "reigns supreme and the tempestuous sea clashes against the steadfast cliffs." It is easy to think such majestic thoughts as the landscape lends itself to such eloquence. I smile to myself.

As we assemble again, a motley crew, our faces etched with lines of determination and uncertainty about the day of filming, the locals emerge, once again, to join us. Unlike most of us, the locals are a strong, hardy breed, born and bred amidst the harsh elements. Armed with shovels and unwavering resolve, they set out to clear the set of the relentless snow that has blanketed the ground, determined to ensure that the magic of cinema will not be thwarted by the whims of winter. But it is no easy feat, that I can see.

The snow, like a mischievous child, piling high, threatens to bury the very set upon which we stand. As we look, a few locals come along and brush us with little brooms, whisking snow from our hats and our coats, to keep us from disappearing, too. Each shovel-full of snow propelled into the air is a testament to the locals' tireless efforts as they carve a path through the powdery abyss.

Nature itself, recognizing the magnitude of this moment, reveals a majestic creature emerging from the depths of the surrounding forest. The Canadian moose, with its towering stature and regal antlers, stands watch at the edge of the set, its eyes fixed upon the flurry of activity before it. It's my first time seeing this giant creature. But in its gaze, I sense a quiet curiosity, as if this creature, too, recognizes the significance of the endeavor unfolding amidst the snow-laden landscape.

The locals pause for a moment, their work momentarily forgotten, as they, too, turn their attention to the magnificent beast. A hushed silence descends upon the set, broken only by the distant cry of seagulls and the rhythmic lapping of waves against the shore. It is a moment of communion, a meeting of two worlds, as man and nature stand united in the pursuit of art.

Then, with renewed vigor, the crew and locals resume their tasks, shovels biting into the snow with a resounding thud. The locals, their faces flushed with exertion, work in harmony, their collective efforts transforming the set into a canvas of possibilities. As the last remnants of snow are cleared away, revealing the raw beauty of the Newfoundland landscape, a sense of triumph fills the air. The moose, a silent observer, watches us, its presence a reminder of the untamed wilderness that surrounds us as we take our places and the director calls, "Action!"

The days move on, sunshine filling the horizon, until the following week when it suddenly turns into gloomy days on set—the weather changing on a whim, as if the skies are already helping us unfold the tragedies that lie in the complexity of the story. Intrigue, secrets, sadness, and humor will be revealed in due course. As the actors emerge from their trailers, I can see that their faces are etched with the mood and preparation of the scenes.

I approach the director, the smoke from his cigarette curling lazily through the air. He seems lost in thought, his brow furrowed with a mix of frustration and determination.

"What's going on?" I ask.

"Trouble," he replies, his voice weary before the day has even begun. "We're already behind schedule, the lighting's off, and the damn snow won't stop."

The cinematographer, a man of few words but deep vision, joins our conversation.

"We need to capture the essence of this place," he says, his voice crisp and purposeful. "The fog, the waves crashing against the rocks, the abandoned ships. It's all part of the tapestry. We need to make the audience feel the weight of this haunting landscape, but now the weather has turned again on us."

We spend the day battling the elements, the fog swirling around us like a shroud, the wind howling through the streets. But each shot is painstakingly crafted, the lighting carefully adjusted to convey the mystery and melancholy that permeates this town. The dialogue crackles with sharp wit and veiled threats as the characters navigate their way through a labyrinth of secrets and lies.

CHAPTER 3

James and I are getting to know each other between filming and weekends, so on this particular day, he invites me out to a late lunch/early dinner. The restaurant is on top of a hill overlooking the bay. The view is spectacular with windows all around. Adirondack chairs decorate the deck, and inside the restaurant, it is warm and sunny. The room is decorated simply with comfortable chairs and white tablecloths.

As our eyes met, a palpable electricity crackles through the air, inviting us closer, like magnets irresistibly drawn together. I exchange a hesitant smile, words unnecessary in this moment of shyness that transcends the boundaries of language. I can feel James studying me with an artist's eye. I have worn my hair in soft waves, framing my face for the early evening out. He looks happy to see me as we take off our winter coats.

We take our seats and look out at the bay. A Titanic-sized iceberg in the distance drifts by, and we become aware of the strains of Celtic music. A local band is playing, and they are called 'What 'Cha 'Ma Call 'Em', as no one can remember their names, only their music. And what music it is! Thrilling in cadence, it is the heart and soul of sailors of days gone by. My ancestors, traders of the sea, have sung the same song in centuries gone by. It echoes in my heart and in my soul. My eyes well up with tears, unexpectedly, and my fingers begin to drum to the tune.

"Have you always lived here?" I ask James.

He smiles at me. "Yes, this has always been home, but I left for a while to study art," he says. "I've been back for five years now and have been teaching art at the school."

"My son loves your class. Do you have kids of your own?"

"No, I was married once, but no kids. My wife died some years ago. Just after we came back."

"I'm so sorry," I murmur, gently.

He hesitates, then continues. "I woke up one morning and she was lying next to me, gone. It turned out to be an aneurism."

I look at him. "Oh, no. How awful for you."

"It's hard when you build your life around someone and then suddenly lose them," he says. He looks out at the bay, again, searching for answers. "I was really lonely for a while. If we'd had kids it might've been different, but she was the only family I had. My parents died young. I guess I had to go out and find another family."

"Another family?" I ask.

"Yes, the kids at the school are my family now, and I've been teaching them for years."

My heart goes out to him. Life throws us many twists and turns.

"And you?" he asks in return. "Tell me about you."

"I was married, too," I reply, "and then divorced. I'm sad to say, my ex is no longer in my son's life very much. He never wanted kids in the first place. It's mainly why we divorced."

"That's a shame," he answers. "I'd have given anything to have had kids. He's missing out."

"Yes, he is," I say, thinking of all the joys my son has brought me over the years.

"It must be hard on your son, too," he adds, gently.

"Yes, it is. I never expected things to turn out this way," I say as our server comes to our table to hand us the menus.

"Hi, folks. What can I get ya?" She has the round, rich voice of the Caribbean, an interesting contrast to this northern place.

"Emma," James asks, "If you're okay with this, I'd like to make a few suggestions? There are a couple of things you should try."

I nod my head, curious to hear what he's going to suggest. James turns to our waitress and points to the menu to let her know what he wants to order, but without saying a word out loud.

"You're being mysterious," I say, puzzled.

"You'll see," he replies.

The waitress winks at me, a big smile on her face. "You're gonna love it," she promises.

We talk for a while, getting to know each other more as we wait for our food.

"Here you go, folks," says our waitress returning, placing hot steaming food before us. "Enjoy!"

The music in her voice lingers and beckons memories of our neighbor, Mama Cunningham, weaving her stories to us as kids on the stoop of her porch in Virginia. Hot summer nights, fireflies, telling us stories in her rich Southern voice, filling our imaginations.

I look at my plate. On it sits cod tongue, a delicacy I'm supposed to try at James's urging. Although little is left, cod is still a symbol of these people's hopes, their land, and their livelihood. The cod tongue is a soft, velvet, gelatinous, melt-in-your-mouth secret of the sea. Strange as it is to me, I like it. A few locals at a nearby table smile and nod approvingly.

"You're officially a Newfoundlander now!" James declares. "Everyone who comes here has to eat this. It's sort of an initiation rite."

Barnacles, another delicacy, are then served after the cod tongue at James's urging. He sees the expression on my face and starts to laugh.

"You have to try them, too," he coaxes.

He picks one up and offers it to me. I bite down cautiously, curiously, as shell, sweet flesh, and salt explode in my mouth. Salty days of my youth in the hot sun, swimming from sunup to sundown, come to mind—clean and fresh, salt and lemons.

But there would be no swimming here. The ocean is already full of mounds of snow, piled up high, as the bulldozers drive the excess snow into the watery wall, pushing hard.

The clinking of cutlery and murmurs of other diners fade into the background as we continue to talk and laugh, drinking a glass or two of wine as we listen to the music. The day passes into night.

"Thank you for a wonderful time," I say as he walks me back to my car and opens the door.

"Let's do it again soon, Emma," he says, bending down to me, his face close to mine. There is a gentleness and warmth in his eyes. Not the usual thing I often see. I begin to feel as though I've known him forever.

"Drive carefully," he adds. "The roads can be slippery."

"I will," I answer. "You, too."

He covers my hand with his and squeezes it.

I arrive home, a smile still on my face. Amber and Noah are just clearing the dinner plates off the table.

"Let's go for a walk," I say, and giggle like a kid. My son's eyes light up and Amber smiles her slow, easy smile.

We are entering the month of "the darling buds of May," but there are no spring buds in sight yet. The snow still stirs around us, staking its frozen foothold into spring. In the spirit of the glistening frost, we decorate a tree outside the house with lights we find and boldly walk around the village in the dark, arm in arm, singing Christmas carols not usually sung in May. Children hear us and begin to follow, hiding behind bushes and rocks, then popping up. We hear and see them laugh and whisper, but we don't care, for it is Christmas once again in our minds and in this crazy springtime.

CHAPTER 4

The next morning around a pancake breakfast at the house, we are startled by the sound of ATVs. There is actually a road nearby we have never seen before. Then, suddenly, we hear another ATV from a different direction. We look out, surprised. We are on a speedway, no longer on an isolated road near a dark, mysterious cemetery. The snow is beginning to melt, and mysteries are being uncovered.

Work continues as planned and things begin to run smoothly. The lighthouse at the bottom of the hill, which seemed so far away and lonely, is stretching its beams closer and closer, welcoming us as though we are starting to belong.

As the weather improves and it begins to warm up slightly, even the actors seem comfortable in their roles and the director has finally relaxed. So, we venture to church. The waves are high, and the winds still warn us to stay home. Ignoring the signs, we bundle up and pile into the car, making our way to the local church.

When we arrive, we find the church is closed. The

locals tell us that the church rotates its services around the island—first in one town, then another—just to fill a few pews each Sunday. The church service wouldn't come back to the same town for at least five or six weeks, perhaps getting lost along the way in the snow. Determined, we chase the service to another village several miles away. By the time we arrive, the Sunday service is in full swing, and we are caught mid-step. The minister, stunned to see new faces, stops in the middle of his sermon and shouts, "Well, hello! Who are you?"

We mumble a response and retreat to the back pew. As we remove our coats and hats, the offering basket suddenly appears in front of us. Embarrassed by our lateness and the public greeting, we stuff as much money into the basket as we can until an usher waves us to stop.

"That's enough!" she whispers as she excitedly whisks the basket away.

The music begins in earnest, and we reach for the worn hymnals in front of us as we stand up to sing. An entire sea of gray and white in front of me is puzzling. It would seem there is no one in the church under the age of sixty. Many of the young people have had to leave to find work elsewhere.

After church, Amber and Noah show me a pathway leading down from the tall cliffs to the ocean. It is a rip-roaring Magic Mountain descent nature has carved for the young at heart. I must try it. I am in a new land—a new found land—where anything is possible, and I feel ten years old. Amber and Noah watch my foolishness, as my bullet-like descent gathers so much speed I am definitely ocean-bound into the icy waters. I imagine their eyes grow bigger and bigger, light-filled circling cartoon orbs, as they watch in alarm. I am in trouble. They run and grab me with all their strength before I, the fool, land in the freezing water.

The climb back up the cliff is deceptively more dangerous than its descent. I have come close to death a few times, and this, apparently, is going to be another one of those times. I have trouble getting back up from the path I have chosen and decide to veer to the right of the path. I climb as high as I can until I am suddenly faced with sheer cliff and the abrupt end of the path. Below me is water with rocks jutting out beneath, and waves that beckon me to jump. The only way forward is to walk backwards and retrace my steps, or to jump straight into the icy water. I feel my heart pounding as my breathing stops. I carefully inch backward, one foot behind the other. I have no other choice. When I finally make it down and back up a different way, the look of terror plastered on my son's face is one I will never forget. God protects fools and the childlike. For what it was worth, I am thankful I stuffed the offering plate at church that morning. Newfoundland is a place to be reckoned with.

CHAPTER 5

I'm also becoming aware of the sheer honesty of these people. In all my years, I have never heard a man say the words, "I don't know." These are such simple words—"I don't know"—but I rarely, if ever, hear a man, especially in the States, (in my experience anyway), say those simple words.

After work, I stop at a market and ask two men for directions, as I am lost. They look at me, then at each other, then turn back to me. Looking me in the eye, one of them says, "I don't know." That short answer is so profound in its simplicity, you could have knocked me over with a feather.

By contrast, at a dinner event back home, months later, I asked a general question of the dinner crowd as to what kind of ducks were portrayed on the paintings on the walls. The men looked, studied the ducks, and each one came back with an answer. It was clear none of them really knew what to say, but culturally, each one felt a need to contribute something, anything. No one had the courage to just say, "I don't know."

That man in Newfoundland took me completely by surprise with his guileless, almost childlike, answer, and plain, direct truth. He didn't know, and he wasn't ashamed to say so. It was as simple as that. *Was this what our ancestors were like a thousand years ago,* I ask myself, *armed with a simple, childlike innocence, unafraid to say they just didn't know?* As a judge I met once in Mississippi said, "Why is everyone afraid to say, 'I don't know?' It's much easier than lying!"

CHAPTER 6

Ahab

We were told of an amazing seafood restaurant in another town. The popular restaurant was buzzing with activity when Amber, Noah, and I got there.. The outside of the building, constructed in an era gone by with its old wooden structure and picket fence, was a reminder of a quaint and quieter time. But now, inside, it is a boisterous place where locals come for conversation and camaraderie. We are seated at a nice table with a view of the water on one side. Yet, amidst the laughter and friendship, in the opposite corner of the room, there broods an undercurrent of melancholy emanating from a sickly-looking man sitting in the shadows alone. He is an unkempt, pale creature, wearing a wrinkled jacket and mismatched pants. His right hand reveals a slight tremor as he twists a fork around and around, surveying the room. He is looking for something, or someone, I can't tell which, his eyes darting from table to table, until his gaze alights on my son.

Then he smiles, his lips curling back to expose

yellowed teeth and his face lights up. He has found who he is looking for. Reaching for an object in the dark corner behind him, he stands up and heads directly our way. A wave of raucous laughter swells up and sweeps across the room. I push back in my chair, instinctively, wanting to keep my distance from this man. Why is he coming towards us? He looks scary, unlike those we've met before in this wonderful place. He has a swagger to his walk, a sway born of a sailor accustomed to life at sea.

He then turns, approaching us from behind, forcing us to turn and look at him. He smells as though he hasn't bathed in a long time. He takes an object he has been carrying close to his side out of the shadows and places it on our table with a careful, yet dramatic, flourish. It is a petrified whale penis about ten feet long.

"This is a whale penis from a real, live whale," he says in too loud a voice.

Amber gasps, her eyes wide with shock. Noah recoils in fear and fascination, while I am stunned into silence.

But there it lay, this silent victim. The man watches our reactions. He knows the power of his prize and is counting on the power of its lure.

Noah's eyes widen in shock, and the man gives Noah a gleeful grin. "Come closer, son," he encourages, as he puts his hands on Noah's shoulders. "Take a look at this beauty. It's a real find, you know. I killed the beast myself."

"Why did you do that?" Amber asks innocently.

"Because it was fun, dear lady," he says. "It was fun! The sport of the kill!"

He looks to almost do a small jig, his shoulders

bobbing up and down.

"Look at the length of it!" he says, his voice now shrill with excitement. "I kilt it!" he says, his pride causing him to slip into old-fashioned speak.

Amber and I look at each other in disbelief. To kill without reason seems unfathomable.

He is Ahab in the flesh. Killing for the sake of killing. If I could, I would physically push him away from us.

I see Noah's eyes widen even more with childlike wonder.

The man stands next to Noah, watching him, and says, "I have some exciting home movies of whales I've hunted you have to see. Come with me, boy." He drops his voice to an urgent whisper and purrs, "Come with me now, and I'll even give you a picture to take home with you."

He puts his hands on Noah's shoulders and begins to massage them. His fingernails are dirty and ragged. "I'll even take you on a boat ride so you can watch the whales swim and you can see how we hunt them." He moves in closer.

"Can I go, Mom?" says Noah, innocently, halfway standing up.

I look at his excited face and the weathered face of this man, with his fish-like eyes. I nod, and Noah stands up, excitedly. But, as I watch them about to leave, my breath catches in my throat. The man seems too eager to take Noah out of the room, and alarm bells start to go off in my head.

"I can teach your whole family how to be rich," he declares, almost as an aside, as he is about to whisk Noah away. "I've made many young boys and their families rich in no time at all," he repeats for extra measure, with a smirk on his face.

"No!" I say, loudly, as I suddenly stand. I don't want to shout around these people I am growing fond of, but the man is too intent in his effort to lure my son away with this bait, and a wave of courage washes over me. The room seems to hush at my outcry; murmurs fade into a collective silence as all eyes turn to witness this unexpected confrontation.

With a mixture of anger and determination, my voice rings out. "Take that object off this table," I say, my tone cutting through the tension. "Now!"

I reach out and grab Noah's hand away from the man's grasp. Diners look on.

"Leave us alone and take that, that...thing with you," I say again.

Amber begins to rise in unity.

The man looks at me, oily and offended, visibly surprised by the force of my reaction. Slowly, inch-by-inch, his hand shaking more than before as if repulsed by its own action, he lifts the prized bait—now insignificant in the face of our defiance—and carefully removes it to his side. The room holds its breath, tension thick in the air, as judgment waits. The man leaves in a huff, carrying the remainder of his twisted intentions away.

Amber sinks back down, and we watch him go, as he retreats, hunched now and angry. We are spared from seeing him again, but are thrown by the exchange and the audacity of his boldness. As the room slowly returns to its normal rhythm, I take my seat once more with a fierce determination to protect my family from any harm that may come their way, no matter what fears or doubts there may be.

Murmurings and subdued conversation begin again as the room starts to return to its previous state.

I turn to Amber as she holds my hand to steady my nerves. "He's gone," she says.

I am grateful she is a defender of rights, too. Noah, sensing danger, looks at me worriedly, but doesn't know why. Quietly and quickly, we finish our meals, cold now, and leave the restaurant.

That night, my son has nightmares and calls out in his sleep. I run to comfort him in the darkness of the house with a new, unwavering determination. As the house quiets down, I look out through the narrow upstairs window in the hallway to the water below. The evening could have turned out so badly. It is unthinkable.

In the dark of night, I watch the lighthouse with its steady beam going round and round. Its steadiness comforts me. Even at a distance, the lighthouse stands tall and proud, a sturdy reminder of the resilience and strength I sense all around me on this island as waves beat and crash against its walls. It is a symbol of these people who have lived lives of waves crashing all around them, but who stand strong in the face of adversity. Its beacon of light pierces through the darkness and cuts through the thick veil of night, offering a sense of reassurance, of safety, and solace to Newfoundlanders against future dangers. The steady rotation of its lighted pulse mirrors the beating of my heart and washes over me like a gentle caress. It is a steadfast guardian that whispers we are not alone—a force greater than our own can be there to guide us through treacherous waters and lead us to safety. Thank God my eyes were opened just in time.

CHAPTER 7

The next day, I have a night shoot so I am free to go with Amber to pick up Noah from school that afternoon. Inside the classroom, I tell James about the man at the restaurant and the alarm bells that went off in my head.

"I may have been wrong, James," I say, "but I didn't feel right, and, you know, for a moment I almost let Noah go with him." I shudder.

He looks at me, carefully, his eyes narrowing and glancing to make sure the children are out of earshot. Then he begins to tell me the story. He knows the man well. "He's known around the area for liking young boys," he says, dropping his voice.

He confirms my fears.

"I feel sorry for his wife," James adds.

"He's married?" I ask, incredulously.

"Yes," he says, "and what a travesty it is. He tries to lure young boys with all sorts of promises, and he promises their families money."

"Then my gut feeling was right," I say. "I'm glad I

didn't let Noah go with him...but I almost did. When I think of how close I came...but there was something in his eyes that made me hesitate."

"You have good instincts," James says.

"No, not always, believe me," I say, ruefully. "But when it comes to my son, I try."

Noah and the kids are almost finished cleaning up and putting their projects away.

"What are you doing this coming weekend?" he asks.

"We were thinking of going sightseeing to watch the puffins," I say.

James smiles. "Let me take you all," he says, reaching for some final brushes to rinse. "I know exactly where to go."

"Oh, that would be great, James. We would love it!" I look at him and smile as my heart tugs a little. Filming in Newfoundland will end soon and we'll have to move to Nova Scotia for some final scenes. I know I will miss him. He is making his way into my heart.

CHAPTER 8

That following Saturday, we bundle up and head for the ocean. When we arrive, the puffins are out en masse. Such colorful birds! James tells us they will be even more colorful when the warmer weather returns and they want to attract mates. They look chubby and round, almost cartoonish.

The puffins are gathered together and then start to fly toward the ocean. The Newfoundland landscape sprawls before us, a remote yet breathtaking sight, as always. The ragged cliffs stand tall, their weathered faces defiantly resisting the relentless assault of the crashing waves. James and young Noah scamper up to a rocky outcrop, their eyes fixated on the puffins. Amber and I watch from below, a short distance away.

We watch the vibrant puffins soaring through the air, their wings painted with a vivid palette of colors.

"Look at them, Noah," James murmurs, a tinge of awe mingling with the deep timbre of his voice. "There's nothing quite like seeing these puffins in flight. They are nature's own little artists."

Noah nods eagerly. "They're cool! And look at how they fly, just like airplanes!" He imitates and follows the birds in colorful formation, his eyes sparkling.

James casts a sidelong glance at Noah as Noah skips along, a flicker of wistfulness dancing in James's eyes. The boy resembles him: the same color eyes, the same hair.

James hangs his head down in thought. "Y'know, Noah," he says, quietly, "I've always wanted a son, someone to share moments like these with." James's eyes scan the horizon.

Noah's gaze turns serious, his young mind grappling with the weight of this man's words and the thrill of this day. "I wish I had a dad like you," Noah says. "Someone who knows things...someone I could have fun with every day!"

A silence settles upon them, both lost in their own thoughts. But amidst the serenity of the landscape, all our attention turns to a solitary puffin, struggling as it swoops down and is suddenly trapped between the unforgiving embrace of the imposing rocks. It flaps its wings furiously as it tries to free itself, its plaintive cries piercing the air, as it calls for freedom.

James glances at Noah, a determined gleam in his eyes. "We can't just stand here, buddy," he says. "Let's try to help that puffin and see what we can do."

With a shared nod, they both set off toward the narrow passage between the rocks, their steps purposeful and resolute.

Amber and I run closer, concerned for their safety.

Try as it might, and flapping its wings furiously, the

puffin is unable to budge. Noah runs up the rocks to the puffin with James following close behind. As carefully as they can, they start to move some of the smaller rocks away. Some of the other puffins circle around.

"Don't worry, Noah," James says, his voice gruff. "We'll free that puffin, the two of us." They work hard moving stones and tangled weeds.

"Almost there," James calls out, his voice tinged with urgency as Noah clears smaller rocks as fast as he can. "We just have to move this big rock…there!"

With one final push, the rock relinquishes its grip, freeing the once-captive wings of the puffin. It soars into the boundless embrace of the sky, a triumphant display of newfound freedom. James and Noah stand side by side, their chests heaving with exertion, their faces illuminated by a shared sense of triumph. The puffin's liberation had become their own. Amber and I begin to breathe again.

Noah turns to James, a wide smile illuminating his young face. "We did it, James!" he exclaims. "We set it free!"

James nods, a hint of vulnerability dancing in his eyes. "Yeah, we did, Noah," he says. "We set it free. Come on, buddy."

As they retraced their steps along the rugged coastline, the wind carried the echoes of their shared victory. In that moment, James realized that the void he had long endured had finally been filled by the bond he had forged with Noah. And Noah, brimming with gratitude, found solace in the paternal figure that James had become. Their shared adventure not only liberated a trapped puffin but also united two lost souls in search of connection. The yearning for a son and the yearning for a father converged in a moment of triumph and unity, etching their shared journey indelibly into the tapestry of their lives.

As they strode, their steps resonating with purpose, James couldn't help but feel a sense of hope flicker within him: the indomitable power of love, unwavering determination, and the unbreakable connection between a father-figure and his son.

CHAPTER 9

The final days of shooting are coming up. Work on set has been good, with bonded friendships and laughter, despite the daily rigors. One night, one of the actors, holding two urns in what was to be a dramatic and somber scene, did everything he could to make the other actor opening the door fall into fits of laughter. She couldn't stop laughing for quite a few takes, and, of course, neither could we. That was the kind of friendship and trust that had developed on set.

The next weekend, James and I head down to the beach again, the sand visible as the snow is finally melting. It's still a cold, windy day, but the air is fresh and invigorating. James sees me shiver and draws me close. The thrill of his arm around me provides comforting warmth.

"You know, Emma," he says as we look out at the water, "several sea battles were fought in Newfoundland over the centuries. Battles between the British and the French primarily. There were ferocious spectacles, with one side winning, then the other. Imagine all those ancient ships out in the ocean firing at each other with their cannons? Ships sank on both sides and with them their treasures, coins, silver, gold, china, and glass."

I listen intently.

"It's not crowded right now," he continues, "because it's still cold weather, but usually there are people out here all the time searching for treasure—sea glass or anything else the water may have given up...even after all this time."

"What a sight it must have been," I remark. "All those ships doing battle so many centuries ago!"

My imagination starts to wander. I imagine ships fighting on the water, and as I look at him, standing there with the wind in his hair, even he looks like a sailor from those many centuries ago. I can just see him standing on the deck of a ship surveying the battle scene.

"Emma, let's look for sea treasure," he offers, taking my hand. The wind picks up, whipping around our coats, but I can feel the heat of his hand in mine beneath the wool, a strong but gentle hand.

As we walk along the beach, I begin to see little pieces of glass embedded in the sand. "Oh look!" I say, as I bend down to pick one up. It is a blue polished gem tumbled by the waters.

"This is sea glass," James informs me. "It's weathered by the sea,"

"It's beautiful," I say, holding it up to the sun. It has a smoky or 'salty' look to it. "I've seen artificial ones in craft stores, but the real thing is so amazing!"

Intrigued, I begin to look for more sea glass. I start to find green ones and more blue ones. Suddenly, I find a small piece of china with a pattern still evident that stops me in my tracks. As I hold it in my hand, I look out at the water, trying to imagine where it might have come from.

It is a small shard of old china, with a delicate pattern still visible despite the centuries it may have spent submerged beneath the waves. In my hands, it holds a story of its own. My eyes light up, and I lose myself in a fantasy of battling ships on the turbulent seas, the sound of cannons booming and the smell of saltwater in the air, china, and precious glass shaking with the firing of the cannons, and now, perhaps, a piece of history in my hand.

As though reading my mind, James begins to recount more of the history. "One of the most significant battles was the Battle of Signal Hill in St. John, Newfoundland in 1762. It involved land and sea battles between the British and the French during the Seven Years' War...plus it was an important battle in the larger sense for control of North America.

"I don't remember learning that part in American history," I say. "Maybe they were simplifying things for us."

"Well, the British were able to seize control of Signal Hill by battling by land and by sea," James continues. "It was a fierce battle. And at one point, the British climbed the cliffs surrounding the fort in a surprise attack to gain control over the French and they succeeded. They say it was then that the world began to realize the importance of naval power in helping to win wars in the struggle for the continent because forces could come in by land as well as by sea. It also gave Britain more control in North America."

"But," I wondered aloud, "if that was in 1762, and the American War of Independence was in 1776, then

Britain's stronger influence in North America must have added to the tensions that were growing between Britain and America. I wonder if it added to our resentment of Britain, and our fight for independence. It's another piece of the puzzle in history that is fascinating."

I didn't remember learning about the Boston Tea Party in quite so clear a way before.

CHAPTER 10

The following day, I am scheduled with work to go out to sea. The ship looks daunting as we step onto it. I am prone to seasickness, despite my seafaring roots, which must have skipped a few generations, but am comforted by the blue skies and the calm ocean. The locals wave at us with big smiles on their faces. They know better; stormy weather lies ahead. We are in for a rough ride and it takes a Newfoundlander or a sailor to know that. In happy ignorance, we wave back.

The medic on board places a box of motion-sickness wristbands on a table for anyone who wants one. I take two, one for each wrist, and some oral medication as well, for good measure. *Better safe than sorry*, I tell myself. Within the hour, I have overdosed on motion sickness medication and think it preferable to throw myself over the railing, followed by a thought that perhaps I should stay on board, alternating with the need to urgently jump overboard and out of my skin. My thoughts swing back and forth like the rocking of the boat, and the water appears, to my crazed mind, to be rising higher and higher as though to help me jump. The medic's appearance stops my racing mind (just as I am on the cycled thought of leaping overboard) as he relays to the hospital to send an ambulance right away to meet us at the dock. The entire ship turns around; I am mortified that the ship and all its passengers have to go back to dock and watch as I am rescued. I am unable to make it down into the small red-and-yellow dingy waiting in the middle of the ocean below like fodder for fish—or as a comedian once said, "like hors d'oeuvres sitting on a Ritz cracker," (referring to airline passengers in safety jackets in a water landing).

Ultimately, eight people abandon ship with me and kiss the ground in gratitude when we dock. For good measure, the stewards have served clam chowder for lunch to the remaining passengers who haven't gone down on the first count. Needless to say, if people haven't thrown up before lunch, they do then. By the end of the trip, we hear that everyone onboard has become sick—save one, lonely, stalwart passenger of Irish seafaring ancestry. This single passenger is the only one left standing on the top deck. It figures; she is not only a person of Irish descent, as are many of these Newfoundlanders, but of strong, hardy stock. With a twinkle in her eye, she smiles the smile of a sea captain, exhilarated by the adventure.

CHAPTER 11

The thick snow crunches on the tires as James and I go over hills to his house. I look at James, and he takes my hand and squeezes it.

"Make yourself at home," he says, as we enter his house.

"This is cozy," I say, looking around, "and nice." Masculine and bold, nature and art have found their way into this home in delightful celebration.

"Thanks," he says. "I'm comfortable here."

He turns on a few lights as dusk approaches. "I'll put the kettle on for some tea in a minute and make a fire. Come on in."

He heads to the dining room, empties his jacket pockets, and puts the pieces of the sea glass he previously collected on our beach walk in the center of the table. On the dining table is a blue glass vase filled with pussy willows and maple leaves; seashells and pinecones are

41

strewn about the table as well. They glisten in the afternoon sun. He looks at me, his eyes sparkling like the sea-glass gems on the table. My breath catches as I look at him.

In the dining room, I find myself surrounded by paintings of indigo ocean waves swirling into each other as they crash along the shore. One could almost hear the sound of the waves as they hit the rocks. I look back at him, thoughtfully. He is a fine painter.

We walk into his kitchen, and he begins preparing some tea. He puts some slices of bread in the toaster.

Reaching for a jar, he asks, "Have you tried our partridge berry jam?"

I look at the purple-colored jam and shake my head.

"It's our local jam. You'll love it," he says. "Here, try some."

He puts some of the jam on a spoon and hands it to me as he takes the toasted bread from the toaster. I taste it and discover its surprise. It is delicious, tart, with just the right amount of sweetness. I find myself delighting more and more in all things Newfoundland. James explains that the berries, which grow wild all over the island of Newfoundland and the continental region of Labrador, are gathered and then simmered in sugar, water, and lemon; most households enjoy making it. But once the berries have burst open, and the aroma fills the kitchen, black tickle molasses from the sap of sugar maple trees is added, giving an additional layer of flavor and sweetness. This is the secret. The black tickle molasses is thick and dark with a caramel-like flavor. The combination creates a sensation of sweetness mixed with tartness that sings on my tongue. What a delightful surprise to the senses!

As James spreads butter and some of the partridge berry jam onto each piece of toast, I wander into the living room to get a closer look at the paintings hanging on the walls. The first painting over the mantle reminds me of springtime. The green of a meadow bursts forth like newly sprung moss after a spring rain, with a sky so clean and fresh. In another, the dark green of the hillside slopes to whisper of a deep forest mysteriously shrouded in gray winter mists. It makes me want to reach out and touch its mystery. Next to it, tall Newfoundland cliffs watch over the land, with giant feet of rock and stone planted solidly in the deep darkness of the water.

On the opposite wall, trees, watching over the bay, some stalwart, some tattered by the wind, seem to march as warriors down to the ocean. In the last, a lone moose looms large and proud gazing over the horizon of the vast Newfoundland waters. Icebergs float in the distance.

"Moose are such strange creatures with their big bodies and spindly legs, aren't they?" I observe, reminded of the description the driver gave when I first arrived. "This one looks like he'd like to tell a joke."

James moves closer to me and smiles. "I think, if you're a moose, you have to have a sense of humor. Just look at those legs!" he says, pointing to the painting.

I look again and laugh. It truly is a curious sight to see, but suddenly, as I look at the moose, a shiver rushes through me. James comes closer and puts his arm around me.

"Are you cold?" he asks.

I shake my head but feel an unexpected chill.

The kettle whistles, jarring me out of the strange feeling, and James heads back to the kitchen. After pouring the tea, he brings the tea tray to the living room. I can smell the perfume of the black tea and the berry jam.

"I'll stoke the fire while the tea steeps," he says, placing the tray on the coffee table. "Have a seat."

I move to the brown leather couch and watch as he makes a fire. His body is tall and lean and muscles ripple under his shirt as he stokes the fire. He hands me a blanket off of the arm of the couch, and I wrap myself in it. The fire starts to crackle and burn, giving off soothing warmth after the outside cold. James sits near me on the couch, and his fingers, clay-soft and cool, gently glide from my hair to my neck and back again as he draws me into a kiss that tastes of sugar and wild berries, warmth and heat.

I shiver again.

"Is anything wrong?" he asks as he continues stroking my hair.

"You're reading me pretty well, James," I answer, "but I better not say what I'm feeling."

"Say it," he urges.

"It's just that we'll be leaving soon, and you'll probably just think of me as 'that crazy American girl who passed through here.'" He looks at me pensively. We kiss again, the taste sweeter than before. Our eyes and hearts fill with possibilities.

CHAPTER 12

The moose encounter is another initiation rite of this faraway land. It is a harsh reality of nature, and few people seem to escape its clutches. Nature, in all of its strength, is a force to be reckoned with, no matter how modern our world.

The children, seated in the back of the van, are mostly spared from the impact of the moose's large body, which is such an otherwise common fatality. And yet, with my son, who is injured, the future is uncertain. I pray and seek comfort as I now stare into the liquid hazel eyes of my son, but he lies there, unseeing.

The accident happened on the way back to the house at dusk after a birthday party. A moose appeared suddenly, and at the highway speed at which they were traveling, the inevitable happened. The driver, one of the mothers from school who had taken the kids out to celebrate her daughter's birthday, didn't stand a chance. According to the RCMP (Royal Canadian Mounted Police), the car must have swerved off the road almost into the ravine to try to avoid hitting the moose. The mother, her daughter, and another little girl, who were all sitting in the front seat, suffered a different fate. The mother died, and the two young girls were badly injured. Amber and Noah were in the back seat.

I reach out to Amber. "How are you? What a relief you're both alive."

"We were really lucky," Amber says. "It happened so fast. There was no time to prepare at all."

"I'm just glad you're okay," I say, hugging her gently. "I'll stay with Noah. I know the doctors want you to stay for observation. Go get some sleep if you can. We should call your parents as soon as possible."

Amber nods and leaves the hospital room. I turn to Noah and stare into his eyes. He looks straight ahead, his eyes unseeing.

"Noah, it's Mommy," I whisper softly. Can you hear me, sweetheart? It's Mommy. Can you hear me?"

No movement.

"Noah? Noah? I miss you, sweetheart. Blink your eyes if you can hear me. Blink...come on, please, blink," I pray. "Can you see me?"

I wait, but there is still no response. His eyes just keep staring straight ahead. I bow my head and pray again. The image of the puffins suddenly come to mind.

"Noah, remember the puffins? Remember how they flew up in the sky? Remember?" I ask. "You liked the puffins flying up in the sky. And you saved the puffin that was stuck. Remember? Blink if you hear me, sweetheart. Come on, blink for mommy. Don't talk, just blink your eyes. Do you see Mommy? Please look at me, sweetheart."

I wait expectantly, barely able to breathe as my throat tightens, looking at him, willing him to blink with all my strength. Those unseeing eyes just stare at me, but then, from a place deep within, they begin to flutter slowly and reach out to me, coming back to life. He blinks, and I begin to kiss him, his hands, and his face as tears run down my cheeks. But no words come out of his mouth, and then he closes his eyes and falls into a deep sleep.

In the silence, I peer out through the darkened window of the hospital, wanting in part to flee this somber room. Night is coming. But in my exhausted mind, there should be no night, only day, only sun, only son, my son. I stand up and move to the window, willing the night away so I can breathe again. I rest my forehead on the cold windowpane to soothe the fear as I look down below. The snow glitters under the lights and whispers to me: *Twinkle, twinkle, little star.*

I turn around and watch my sleeping son, and one saving thought helps me. The thought reminds me that nature is also a force for good. Nature tries desperately to keep us alive, to heal us in any way it can, no matter how hopeless the situation. Nature claws and fights for survival with everything in its power. So, with the last ounce of strength in me, I draw in a deep, uneven breath and with renewed hope, I begin to pray and pray again, urging nature to fight, to fight, to fight with all its might to keep my son alive, and to restore his body and his mind to its precious wholeness. "Please, Lord," I whisper, "answer my prayer." My tears mingle with those of the Newfoundland women whose woven prayers comfort me.

My hands feel the rough warmth of my sweater as I sit,

waiting. The sweater is made of strong Newfoundland wool. The beautiful sea-grey and blue-flecked texture of the wool whispers to me of a winter sea-storm-rich colors born and stirred by the waves of the ocean. Each nub, each stitch bears the thoughts and prayers of every Newfoundland woman, hoping and praying for her loved ones. Sitting vigil by the bedside of a beloved husband or child, these steadfast women weave their silent prayers for healing and life, prayer-by-prayer, stitch-by-stitch. No ordinary sweaters are these. They are woolen rosaries of hope and healing that comfort and bring life.

CHAPTER 13

The next morning, Noah's doctor and a younger doctor come in to examine him and introduce themselves to Amber and me. They both seem compassionate and concerned. After examining him physically, they look at Noah intently, and begin asking him a few questions.

"Where were you yesterday, Noah?" his doctor asks.

Noah stares at the floor.

I shake my head at the doctors.

They see a toy airplane in his hand. "Do you like airplanes?"

Noah looks at the airplane, then looks up at the doctors.

"Noah, do you remember what you did yesterday?"

Noah looks down at the floor again, puzzled.

"Do you remember Bridget's birthday party?" I ask, hopeful.

"Remember we went to Bridget's party?" Amber asks.

Noah just looks ahead.

The doctors write down a few things.

"How old are you, Noah?" the younger doctor asks.

Noah stares and opens his mouth but nothing comes out.

The older doctor holds up his hands. "Are you this much?" he asks, holding up six fingers.

Noah doesn't answer.

"Are you this many?" the younger doctor asks, holding up eight fingers.

Noah gives an almost imperceptible nod.

"Good boy, Noah," he says, and pats him gently on the shoulder.

"What's happened to his speech?" I ask. "Will he get it back?"

The doctors look at me before answering.

"We've diagnosed him with transient aphasia," one of the doctors says, "which means he's experiencing a temporary loss of language function. But the good news is that with the right treatment, he should be able to recover fully."

They go on to explain the various treatments they will be prescribing, including speech therapy, cognitive exercises, and medication to help improve blood flow to the brain.

Over the next few days, Noah underwent a series of tests and evaluations to determine the extent of his condition. At first, progress was slow, and Noah became frustrated with his inability to communicate. But his doctors and therapists were encouraging, and they helped him stay motivated and focused on his recovery.

Slowly, but surely, Noah began to make progress. His words became slightly clearer, though still jumbled. He was able to understand the words of others and was trying to respond.

The doctors continue to monitor his progress and adjust his treatment as needed. They prescribed additional medication to help manage his symptoms and referred him to a neurologist for further evaluation.

"He's had an injury to the head, so it seems he may have temporary loss of memory caused by the accident," his doctor explains. "We're going to run some tests. Hopefully, he'll be fine once he's had a chance to recover and the swelling's gone down."

I turn to Amber. "I'm so thankful you're both alive," I say again.

"I know," Amber says, "it could've been much worse. It just happened so fast. One minute we were driving down the road singing songs, and the next minute we were hit."

"Are you going to be okay?" I ask, concerned.

"I'm fine," she replies, then turns and reaches for Noah's hand.

The younger doctor smiles at her. "I'm glad you were spared," he says.

Amber blushes.

I am so grateful, and also so worried about what the tests might reveal.

James and two of the other teachers arrive to check in on Noah and his two hospitalized classmates.

James comes in and crosses over to me, taking my hand as he looks at Noah.

"Hey there, bud. How are ya?"

Noah looks at him.

"How is he?" James asks.

"Okay," I say. "He was lucky, but he isn't talking much. The doctors are going to run some more tests."

James grabs my hand and squeezes it tightly. "He's going to be fine, don't worry."

I look up at him and nod.

"I was sad to hear about Bridget's mother," he whispers. He reaches for his backpack and takes out a bag filled with homemade cards and notes from the students in art class, then hands them to Noah.

"Noah, these are for you from your classmates," James says. "They're get-well cards. All the kids are asking about you and they all hope you'll get better really soon so you can play with them."

Noah takes the bag and reaches in for a card. I have tears in my eyes. He looks at them, blankly.

"We'll open them tomorrow," James offers.

Noah closes his eyes. It's been an overwhelming day. James looks at him and puts the cards at the foot of his bed.

"And now that he's going to sleep, why don't you close your eyes for a bit?" he offers. "Tomorrow, some of the kids may be coming by to visit Noah."

I am touched to hear that.

"I'll come back tomorrow, too, and stay longer. You rest now, while you can." He kisses me and looks again at Noah as he leaves with a wave to Amber, who is sitting on the spare bed looking at one of the cards.

When Noah wakes up, we open some of the cards just before dinner. There is no emotion in Noah's face, yet we persevere. When we tape the cards around the room, they look colorful and bright, and the room instantly feels more cheerful.

The next day, James returns.

"Thank you for the cards," I say, as I kiss him on the cheek. "I think they made him happy."

"I'm glad," he says. "The kids seemed happy to do it."

He then unloads his backpack filled with art supplies. "Noah, look what I have here!"

I can see on Noah's face that he doesn't register what the paints are for, so James shows him, patiently. He lines the paint tubes, one by one on the bedside table, and they start painting together, with James guiding Noah's hand at first. Noah looks intent and his hand is unsteady. James slowly shows Noah how to paint a puffin. First, he shows him by painting one, and says, "See Noah, this is a puffin!"

I look up at James, and I start to understand his intention. He wants to help Noah remember by painting if he can, so he will remember and process what happened as gently as possible.

"Art therapy?" I ask.

"Something like that," James grins.

Noah, concentrating hard, begins painting with James who guides his hand, first dipping the brush into the water, then the watercolors, and back again onto the paper. I sit on the chair and pretend to read, stealing glances at both of them now and then. But unlike his pictures from before, these paintings are scratch-like, scribbling almost. James looks concerned, but only I see his worry. He hands Noah another piece of paper, and Noah draws again.

The doctors come back later that morning. "The x-rays reveal he still has some pressure on the front of the brain from the accident," they explain. "He needs an operation to relieve some of the swelling. He's had a concussion and fluid is building up."

I begin to shake. I look at Noah and stroke his arm gently.

"We'd like to operate tomorrow. We'd rather not delay with this."

"Tomorrow?" I ask, surprised.

"Yes, the sooner the better. Amber is free to go home or stay at the hospital until tomorrow. She is doing fine."

But Amber wants to stay for the operation and beyond, as necessary.

The next morning, we wait anxiously, while the doctors perform the operation. The doctors have reassured me that this isn't a complicated surgery, but a necessary one. We pray and wait, terrified he is going through this. We continue to wait and eventually the doctors come out. The operation is a success. He isn't able to sit or walk for a while, but slowly he regains his gait and we start to work with him. The doctors suggest with my speech degree that I take the time to reteach him and remind him how sounds are made. Amber offers to help as well, as she has the patience of Job having been raised in a big family of eight children. We begin working with him as the doctors and nurses taught us before leaving the hospital.

The following day, as the doctors predict, the swelling goes down, and his power of speech begins to return. Primarily, he seems to have lost his recollection of the events shortly before and during the accident. But, we are so grateful to have him back.

"He wants to see his dad, Amber," I whisper to her. "I've been trying to contact him."

Later that day, when Noah is asleep, I try to reach his father again but without any luck. A few days later, he returns my call and I explain what has happened.

"So, Miles, can you fly up and see Noah? He's asking for you."

"No, it's not possible with work," Miles answers, then sniffles, a habit of his when he isn't telling the truth.

My heart sinks. "He's going to be disappointed," I say. "He's been through a lot and wants to see you."

"Sorry, no can do," he replies, sniffling again. "But let me know how he's doing….oh, and bring him over to come and see me when you both get back," he adds. An afterthought.

And then, "I've gotta go." His famous recurring line.

The connection goes dead. I turn off my cell phone, and go back to the hospital room, curling up next to Noah, who still seems to be asleep. I tell Amber his dad isn't coming. She is shocked by the news and looks at Noah, who stirs in his sleep.

"Poor kid," she says.

Sometime later, Amber goes back to the house. I fall asleep next to Noah, awaking the next morning with a text from his father: "I've changed my plans," it reads. "Catching a plane tomorrow."

CHAPTER 14

Noah wakes up to the sound of my moving around the room. The pale blue walls and the array of medical equipment surrounding him start to make him feel anxious and confused despite the well-meaning cards. I sit back beside him on the bed, holding his hand and try my best to comfort him.

"It's going to be okay, Noah," I say softly, willing my voice to show reassurance. "The doctors are doing everything they can to help you and we're going to be leaving soon."

Noah is excited when he sees Amber and James come into the room, followed by people from school and the town, with children carrying balloons, toys, and more get-well cards to fill the room. Suddenly, there is an overwhelming feeling of love and support. It touches us deeply.

Noah's eyes widen with joy as his friends and neighbors gather around his bed, each with a warm smile on their face.

"Hey, Noah!" says his classmate, Jace. "We brought

you some balloons and some of your favorite superhero action figures. We hope they make you feel better!"

Noah's face lights up as he receives the gifts, and says, "Hi!" to Jace.

Susan, the school's librarian, speaks next. "We made you a card, Noah, with people from the community who signed it and wrote you special messages. We're all rooting for you!"

Noah opens the card, and we read each heartfelt message, our eyes filling with gratitude and happiness.

"Noah," she adds, "we want you to know that you're not alone in this. We're all here to support you and help you get back on your feet."

Noah smiles from ear to ear.

The townspeople take turns sharing stories, telling jokes, and making Noah laugh. They create a lively atmosphere in the room, helping Noah forget about his pain, even if just for a little while.

Alex, another one of Noah's classmates, chimes in. "Noah, we're all planning a special surprise for you once you're out of the hospital. We're going to have a big party with games, cake, and lots of fun!"

"Oh, wow, for me?" Noah asks excitedly. "I can't wait!"

The room fills with more laughter and excitement as they discuss the details of the upcoming party. James, Amber, and I watch with pride as the community comes together to bring joy to Noah's life. I've never seen anything quite like it before.

James takes his hand. "Noah, remember that we're here for you every step of the way. Whenever you need someone to talk to or to play with, we're all just a phone call away."

Noah looks at him gratefully.

Everyone then joins hands, forming a circle around Noah's bed. They close their eyes and offer a heartfelt prayer for his quick recovery. The room is filled with hope, goodwill, and a sense of unity. *Oh, Newfoundland, land that I love.*

CHAPTER 15

B ut the next day, tears well up in Noah's eyes as he struggles to express himself. He doesn't believe his dad is coming. Noah looks up at me, hurt evident in his gaze. His voice quivers as he speaks through tear-filled eyes.

"No! He's too busy," he says. "You told Amber."

My heart aches for him. I reach out to gently stroke his hair, attempting to offer some solace.

"He's coming, Noah. I promise," I assure him. "He texted because he realizes how important it is to be here for you."

We focus on the routine of the day until finally Noah sleeps again, and I go out to the hallway to check my messages. I get another message from Miles. He's not coming. "Something came up. Can't make it after all."

I see James coming down the corridor. We hug and kiss in the hallway, and he hands me something to unwrap. It's a picture he drew of a heart with a teardrop in the middle of it, and looking from above is an angel with the words printed, *No teardrop is ever wasted, for every drop that falls, angels run down to count and keep record.* James has painted it with thought and care, a keepsake forever. We kiss again. But James can see I am sad. The atmosphere suddenly shifts, as we see Miles standing there.

"How's Noah?" he asks, quickly..

"Not too good today," I reply.

The door opens, and Amber comes out. "He seems more confused than he has been. I think he's anxious for Miles."

Noah's eyes open, and his gaze shifts to James. "Dad," he says, his eyes searching for reassurance. He attempts to speak and reach out with his hands, but his words come out jumbled, leaving him frustrated once again. James approaches the bed, reaching out to take Noah's outstretched hand in his own, trying to bridge the confusion between them.

"I'm here, Noah. I'm sorry I wasn't here earlier, buddy." He looks at Noah, concerned.

"Sweetheart," I say, gently, "your dad couldn't make it. Something came up. Maybe he'll come again later."

Noah's disappointment is palpable. He pulls his hand away from James's grasp and turns his gaze away, the hurt evident on his face.

"Too late," Noah murmurs, his words clear again, but barely audibly carrying a weight of disappointment.

My heart aches as I witness the emotional turmoil and feel my own guilt. I try my best to comfort both of them, but the tension in the room lingers, leaving an unspoken heaviness in the air.

But James, cleverly and with patience, begins to talk

with him about school, his friends, and even the puffins. Slowly, Noah's confusion lifts, and he is able to see that it is James who is here, and they begin to share their common memories and laughter. Noah suddenly realizes this man is a better father than his own. He is kind, gentle, and genuinely caring.

CHAPTER 16

We return to the house the following week. Noah's speech is clearer; he is improving and luckily we have a two-week break before moving to Nova Scotia for the final scenes of the film.

James visits Noah in his room and gives him a huge paintbox set. Noah gasps. "For me?"

"Yes," James says, "this is your own special set. Look at all the colors. See? And you can mix plenty more and create some new ones like I showed you." James pats Noah on the back, affectionately.

"James" Noah begins, "there's something I've got to tell you." Noah reaches under his pillow and takes out a tube of paint and a paintbrush. "I took these from you. I'm sorry."

"I wondered where these were. Why did you do that, Noah?"

"I don't know. I guess I just wanted to keep them."

"Noah, it isn't right to take something that's not yours."

"I know. I'm sorry." Noah hesitates for a moment, then reaches for the paint set and hands it back. "I did something bad. Here, I shouldn't have this."

"No, you keep it, son. I want you to have it."

"Really? Thanks, James."

James gently pats Noah's back again, and says, "Hey! Are you hungry?"

"I guess I am," Noah gives a little laugh of relief.

"Let's go see what your mom and Amber are cooking up in the kitchen. It smells good." As James walks out the bedroom door, Noah stands for a second, hesitates, then reaches for the paint set to take downstairs. James pokes his head back in, and says, "Come on, Noah. Let's go!"

Noah is excited to show me his present from James. "Look, Mom! Look what I got. It's a paint set just for me!" I look up at James, gratefully.

"You know what I'm gonna do? I'm gonna sleep with it right under my pillow, and paint all day, James!" Noah says, as he stuffs his face with a cookie and proudly carries the paint box back up the stairs. I give James a hug, and Amber offers him the biggest cookie on the tray.

CHAPTER 17

The following week, a curious thing happens on set. We have taken time out to audition an actress who has flown up from New York, but her audition is not going well. I stand on set, in the dark, to one side. The casting agents and director exchange disappointed glances as the actress struggles to grasp the essence of the character, failing to deliver the required emotions. There are beats and transitions, but she is not hitting any of them. I know the lines by heart as I have played her part, coaching the actors in the scenes time and again. Our director is trying to be patient, but the actress keeps missing beat after beat—puzzling, as she is an experienced actress.

"Alright, let's give it another try! Action!" the director calls out.

The scene begins again, but the actress continues to miss every beat, leaving the set filled with an awkward silence as people look around. The casting directors and director trade concerned looks, unsure of how to proceed.

"Okay, let's give it one last shot," our director says.

It's getting to the end of our film shoot, and this does not bode well. It will take time to fly another actress up to Newfoundland with visas, costumes, contracts, and all that it would entail. She is a well-known actress with a good reputation, but her performance is perplexing to all of us. The actors are baffled because her reputation has been solid thus far. They reluctantly give her one last chance and set up again, but we've already been through several takes. Sure enough, her performance falls flat once again. The room grows tense as glances of frustration and disappointment are exchanged openly.

"Thank you for your efforts. We'll be in touch," the director says as gently as possible, kneeling down and keeping his voice low. The actress nods. She knows she has missed the mark and is crestfallen. She leaves quietly.

The casting agents and director ponder their next move, realizing they need someone capable of bringing the character to life, and that they need to find someone as quickly as possible.

With no answers and everyone confounded, we all leave to go home at the end of a long day while the director and actors consult with studio heads.

CHAPTER 18

S itting in my room later that night, my phone rings suddenly, interrupting my thoughts. It's the director on the other line.

"Emma, we've been discussing the role, and we believe you're the one who can do it justice. Will you take over the part?"

My eyes widen with surprise and delight.

"Me?" I ask in disbelief. "Are you serious?" I repeat, sitting up. It has been a long time since I have acted.

"Absolutely," he continues. "We believe in your talent and the actors want you as well as the studio. Can you be on set tomorrow morning for a rehearsal?"

"Yes, I'll be there," I say, determinedly. "And thank you so much for this chance," I add, hardly able to breathe.

To prepare for the scene, the actors generously give their time and expertise in helping me. It's one thing to be coaching someone on the sidelines and quite another to be acting opposite them in a film.

"When was the last time you were on camera?" asks

the actor who will be playing my husband.

"Don't ask," I say, nervously. "Ask me when the scene is done!"

The director is very solicitous, providing me with notes I may need before we start. The cameramen help me with the exact positioning. *What more could I ask for?* And, like riding a bike, it all starts to come back to me, slowly—and then I pick up speed.

The following week, I leave Amber and Noah to see my father. I have received word he is dying, and the studio has let me leave, especially now as we are on a temporary hiatus.

As I stand by his bedside, and we talk briefly, the weight of the moment weighs heavily on my shoulders. My father, once a tall oak tree, looks up at me, the light fading from his loving, intelligent eyes. I reach for his hand, wanting to give him the gift of good news. It's all I have to give.

"Dad, I have something to tell you. I got a principal part in our film last week."

My father's face lights up with a mixture of joy and pride, his voice barely a whisper.

"I'm...so...glad," he says, slowly, with painful effort. It is a God-given moment.

My eyes well up with tears as I realize this opportunity is more than just a career milestone. It is a sign that my father's support and belief in my dreams have been guiding me all along. This is the greatest gift from God I could give him back in return.

I knew the world would never be the same without his presence. The world was losing a wonderful man. He died that night.

A heavy fog greeted me the next morning, and looking up, with a heavy heart, the sky seemed dark and sad.

We have three more days of shooting in Newfoundland before going to Nova Scotia to finish the final scenes of the movie. James, Amber, Noah, and I decide to take a walk after supper. It was meant to be an ordinary farewell walk into town, with no expectations beyond enjoying the beauty. As we stroll along the rugged shoreline, a sense of tranquility envelopes us. The rhythm of the waves crashing against the rocks and the gentle breeze whispering through the trees creates a symphony of serenity. Our anticipation grows as we approach a secluded spot, where the cliffs offer an unobstructed view of the vast ocean. Suddenly, the stillness is shattered by an explosive burst of water and a resounding splash. Startled, we turn our attention toward the source of the commotion.

To our astonishment, a pod of whales appears, breaching the surface in a spectacular display of power and grace. The air is filled with a mix of exhilaration and awe as the massive creatures leap out of the water, their majestic bodies suspended momentarily in mid-air before plunging back. We stand in that moment, our eyes full of wonder.

Amber turns to Noah and whispers, "Noah, can you believe what we're seeing? It's like magic!"

James, who has been silently observing the scene, steps forward and holds my hand. "This is pretty amazing, isn't it, Emma? You won't find this in your own backyard."

"I know," I reply quietly. "This moment, right here, it really is magic."

"You're right, Emma," he says. "Sometimes, the most magical experiences are the ones that take us by surprise."

Then, going down on his knee, James asks, "Emma, will you marry me?"

Hearing this proposal, Amber and Noah looked at each other, their faces glowing with surprise and happiness.

"Yes! Yes, I will! I don't want to ever leave you or this beautiful place! But... " I hesitate, "...if it snows this much again, will you be able to find me?"

"I'm a Newfoundlander! With the tenacity and courage of my Irish ancestors!" James announces boldly. "Of course, I'll find you!" He jumps up and hugs me, laughing.

As the whales continue their graceful dance in the ocean, the four musketeers we have just become stand captivated, both by the spectacle before us and by what lies ahead. In this moment, our belief in magic becomes more than just a concept; it becomes a tangible reality. We realize that magic is not just limited to fairy tales and fantasy, but it can be found in the marvels of nature and the unexpected adventures life has in store.

CHAPTER 19

As the sun dips below the horizon, casting a blood-red glow across the ocean, our director calls it a wrap for our last day in Newfoundland. We gather together, cast and crew, exhaustion etched on our faces, but a glimmer of satisfaction in our eyes. We had captured the essence of a dark and brooding world, blending it seamlessly with the rugged beauty of Newfoundland. As I walk away from the set for the last time, the fog rolling in behind me, I can't help but think that the essence of Newfoundland, a place where the shadows dance and the truth lies buried somewhere beneath the waves, is now in our souls. All that I have been through here has given me a newfound strength I never knew I had.

As our time in Newfoundland came to an end, people throughout the village came to the house, ringing our doorbell to say goodbye. The landscape is no longer a sea of frozen white, but dotted with bright colors, bobbing hats and laughter. Some people bring gifts of books and homemade cards. The children have all written letters to my son who is healing well. A young woman and her mother stayed up half the night making partridgeberry jam for us. Another family baked bread.

We are forever touched by the actions of these wonderful people and the memories live in our hearts for a lifetime. What a kind, gentle people are these Newfoundlanders. How blessed we were to have been there. And soon it would be home.